50p

A SURPRISE FOR MRS PINKERTON-TRUNKS

MORE STORIES FROM 'GET UP AND GO'

Shirley Isherwood

Illustrated by Maureen Roffey

HUTCHINSON
London Melbourne Sydney Auckland Johannesburg

BY THE SAME AUTHOR

Is that you, Mrs Pinkerton-Trunks?

Hutchinson Children's Books Ltd

An imprint of the Hutchinson Publishing Group

17–21 Conway Street, London W1P 6JD

Hutchinson Publishing Group (Australia) Pty Ltd
16–22 Church Street, Hawthorn, Melbourne, Victoria 3122, Australia

Hutchinson Group (NZ) Ltd
32–24 View Road, PO Box 40-086, Glenfield, Auckland 10

Hutchinson Group (SA) Pty Ltd
PO Box 337, Bergvlei 2012, South Africa

First published 1985

Text and illustrations © Yorkshire Television 1985

Set in Baskerville by Book Ens, Saffron Walden, Essex

Printed and bound in Great Britain by Anchor Brendon Ltd,
Tiptree, Essex

British Library Cataloguing in Publication Data

Isherwood, Shirley
A surprise for Mrs Pinkerton-Trunks.
I. Title   II. Roffey, Maureen
823′ .914[J] PZ7

ISBN 0-09-160380-3

Contents

A Surprise for Mrs Pinkerton-Trunks

This is a story about a little girl called Billie and her wonderful dog, Woodley, and her three special toys, Mr Milford-Haven the lion, Mrs Pinkerton-Trunks the elephant, and little Monkey.

It was Mrs Pinkerton-Trunks's birthday, so Billie decided to have a party for her in the garden.

'What shall we eat?' said Monkey.

'Mrs Pinkerton-Trunks must choose,' said Billie, 'because it's her birthday.'

Mrs Pinkerton-Trunks was very pleased to be having a party. But she couldn't make up her mind what kind of sandwiches to have. She went for a long walk to help her to think. Billie and the animals sat on the bench, and watched her. Round and round the garden she went.

'I think cheese sandwiches would be nice,' she said as she went by. But when she came round again, she said, 'Lettuce and tomato are nice, too – I just can't make up my mind which to choose!'

'Mrs Pinkerton-Trunks,' said Billie, when Mrs Pinkerton-Trunks came by again, 'why don't you have cheese sandwiches – *and* lettuce and tomato sandwiches?'

'Or,' said Woodley, 'you could have sandwiches with all three things in together.'

Mrs Pinkerton-Trunks sat down on the grass, and sighed. 'Oh, dear,' she said, 'it is very difficult to choose. Now I don't know whether to have cheese sandwiches, and lettuce and tomato sandwiches – or sandwiches with all three things in together!'

'Well, I don't care for cheese,' said Mr Milford-Haven, and that settled the matter. They would have two plates of sandwiches – one with cheese, and one with lettuce and tomato.

Choosing just where in the garden to have the party was more difficult.

First of all Mrs Pinkerton-Trunks said that she would like to have her party beneath the tree –

but when she walked to the top of hill, she sat down and sighed again. 'The view is delightful,' she said, 'But it might be nice to have my party near the flower-beds, so that I can smell the flowers.'

She walked back down the hill and sat on the bench. Monkey came and sat by her side. 'I just can't choose,' said Mrs Pinkerton-Trunks. 'You choose for me, dear.' 'The tree!' said Monkey. 'Then we can sit in the shade.'

So the cloth was laid beneath the tree, and the sandwiches, the jelly and the birthday cake were laid out. Everything looked wonderful, and Mrs Pinkerton-Trunks was very pleased. She walked back to the house to put on her hat and Billie saw her stop from time to time to smell the flowers in the flower-beds. And so, as a surprise, Billie decided that she would put a big bowl of red flowers in the middle of the cloth. She sent everyone off to see what they could find.

Woodley came back with a bunch of poppies. Mr Milford-Haven brought roses, and Billie and Monkey staggered up with a big pot of geraniums. But which to choose?

'My poppies,' said Woodley. 'They are the same red as Mrs Pinkerton-Trunks's hat.'

'But the geraniums are bigger,' said Monkey.

Billie put the pot in the middle of the cloth, and everyone stepped back to look.

'It's much *too* big!' said Woodley, 'There's no room for the cake!'

So Mr Milford-Haven's roses were put in the middle of the cloth.

It was a lovely party. 'I've enjoyed every minute of it, dear!' said Mrs Pinkerton-Trunks, as everyone made their way home.

'The sandwiches were very tasty,' said Mr Milford-Haven.

' . . . and I've never seen such a red jelly,' said Monkey.

' . . . or such a beautiful cake,' said Woodley.

' . . . and the scent of the roses was simply delightful!' said Mrs Pinkerton-Trunks.

The Box House

One day, Billie made a house on the top of the hill. She called it her box house, because it was made from a big cardboard box.

When she had made her house, she decided that she would make some curtains for the windows. She went back to the kitchen, and made her curtains from some old Christmas paper. Then she decided that she would paint some wallpaper – so she got out her paint jars and her two brushes. Then, together with Woodley, Mrs Pinkerton-Trunks, Mr Milford-Haven and Monkey, she climbed back to the top of the hill.

But when Billie hung the curtains at the

windows, they were much too long. So she knelt on the floor, and cut off a strip – and then another strip, until they were just the right length.

When Billie had hung her curtains, she took her brush and began to paint some broad yellow stripes on the walls. Mrs Pinkerton-Trunks came to help, and painted some green wavey lines next to the broad yellow stripes. Monkey became so excited by the painting that Billie let him dip his paw in the yellow paint, and make some thin stripes, next to the broad stripes and the green wavey lines.

'Here's a good design!' said Woodley, and he dipped his paw in the blue paint, and began to make paw-marks on the broad yellow stripes.

Mr Milford-Haven watched for a while, then he said, 'What it needs is a *big* paw-mark – first a little paw-mark, and then a big paw-mark.'

Billie watched Woodley and Mr Milford-Haven making paw-marks, then she dipped her hand into the blue paint and made the shape of it on the wall. She made hand-shapes right up the wall and across the ceiling. When she had finished, she sat down with the animals to admire the work. Their hands and paws were covered with every colour of paint, and they held them out to show one another.

'I've got rainbow paws!' cried Monkey, 'Rainbow paws!' and he ran out of the house and down the hill, leaping and shouting.

'He's a bit over-excited,' said Woodley. As he spoke, he noticed that his tail wa hanging in the jar of blue paint. He took it out and shook it, splattering drops of blue all over the wall.

'Interesting colour for a tail,' said Mr Milford-Haven,' 'Don't know anyone who has a blue tail.' Woodley was very pleased and proud. He strolled out and down the hill, waving his blue tail.

Mrs Pinkerton-Trunks came to sit down beside Billie. 'Would you like a nice green wavey line painted on your forehead, dear?' she asked.

'Yes!' said Billie, and she lay back, and pushed her hair out of the way. But before Mrs Pink-erton-Trunks could paint the wavey line, Mr Milford-Haven said, 'Why is Monkey hanging in mid-air like that? It's a bit odd . . . .'

Everyone turned to look – and there was Monkey, hanging in the doorway, his rainbow paws dangling in front of him. Holding him by the scruff of the neck was the hand of Billie's father. 'What *are* you doing?' he asked. 'And what has happened to Monkey's paws?'

'We've been decorating my box house,' said Billie. 'We've made some curtains, and painted some wallpaper.'

Billie's father put Monkey down on the ground and bent to look inside the house. He looked at the curtains, and the walls – then he looked at the floor where Billie and the animals sat in a mess of torn paper and spilled paint. Then he looked at Billie and the animals, and at their yellow, blue and green hands.

'Bath time!' he said.

'But we haven't had our tea!' said Billie.

'Bath time!' said her father.

Sadly, Billie and the animals made their way down the hill. As they went down they passed the pond, and saw Woodley sitting by the water's edge, dipping his tail amongst the lily-pads. At the bottom of the hill, they turned and looked back at their box house one last time before going in for their baths.

'Never mind, dear,' said Mrs Pinkerton-Trunks. 'The wallpaper is lovely, and the curtains are delightful . . . and we can always come back tomorrow – and paint some roses round the door!'

Morning Comes

One morning, Woodley jumped up on to Billie's bed and tugged at her bedclothes. 'Wake up!' he said. 'I want to show you something in the garden!'

Billie got out of bed and opened the curtains. 'There's nothing there,' she said. 'Nothing's happening!'

'The morning's going to happen,' said Woodley, 'that's what I want to show you.'

Billie put on her red wellingtons and her coat, and went down into the kitchen where the animals lay sleeping in the wagon.

'Wake up!' she said. 'The morning's going to start!' But Mr Milford-Haven and Mrs

Pinkerton-Trunks just went on snoring, and Monkey snuggled deeper into his blue blanket.

Billie took hold of the wagon string and went out into the garden with Woodley, pulling the sleeping animals behind her. Everything was very still and quiet. 'Where are the birds?' said Billie.

'Asleep,' said Woodley.

Billie looked at the shadowy hill. She couldn't see the grass, or the hole where the rabbit lived. She bent down and shook Mr Milford-Haven. 'Wake up!' she said. 'You'll miss the morning!'

Mr Milford-Haven opened an eye and looked at her. 'Wouldn't miss that for anything,' he said – then he closed his eye and began to snore again.

Billie got up and went to look at the flowers – but they were all tightly closed.

'The flowers are asleep!' she said.

She went to look at the pond, but there were no ripples on the water.

'The fish and the frog are asleep,' said Woodley.

'Wake them up,' said Billie. 'I want the morning to start.'

Woodley dipped his paw in the pond and stirred the water, but no fish or frogs appeared.

Billie went to the wagon and shook Mrs

Pinkerton-Trunks. 'Wake up!' she said. But Mrs Pinkerton-Trunks just said, 'Yes, dear – very nice, dear,' in her sleep; and Monkey snuggled so deep inside his blanket that all that could be seen of him was the top of his head.

Woodley ran to the top of the hill and sat down. As he waited, the sky grew lighter and lighter. First it became a deep blue, and then a pale blue – then it became red – and pink – and gold.

'Cheep!' said a bird in a tree.

Woodley ran back down the hill. 'Here comes the morning!' he said.

Ripples went across the pond as the fish came to the top of the water. The frog jumped from the reeds and said, 'Rivett!' All the birds in the trees began to sing.

'Wake up!' said Billie. 'Animals, wake up! You're missing the morning!'

Monkey awoke, and scrambled from his blanket. Mrs Pinkerton-Trunks opened her eyes, and Mr Milford-Haven yawned and stretched. Then he leapt from the wagon, and padded over the grass. He put his head in the bush, to wake up any creatures who might still be asleep. 'Look alive in there!' he said. 'The morning's started!' When he came back to Billie, his paws and mane were all wet with dew.

Mr Milford-Haven was pleased and surprised.

'I'm covered in little drops!' he said. 'Little sparkley drops!'

Billie stared at him. He looked very beautiful, as though he were covered in diamonds. Then he shook himself, and began to climb the hill.

Billie and the animals followed, and everyone stood and watched the sky, until it was time for breakfast.

Mrs Pinkerton-Trunks
and the Baby

One sunny day in the garden, Billie sat down in her little red wheelbarrow. 'It's like being in a pram!' she said to Woodley.

Woodley was lying in the doorway of his kennel, and he opened an eye and looked at her. 'Pram?' he said. 'A pram? You don't need a pram – you're not a baby!'

'I'm pretending to be a baby,' said Billie. 'A tiny, little baby.' Then she curled up, closed her eyes, and fell asleep.

Billie had not been asleep long, when she awoke – suddenly – for she was being wheeled along the garden path, going bumpety-bump over the stones and hollows. Billie sat up, and looked over the side of the wheelbarrow, and saw the flower beds, the pond and the bench going past; then she bent and looked down between the handles of the wheelbarrow, and saw that Mrs Pinkerton-Trunks was pushing as hard as she could. 'Oh, it's so nice to have a little baby to look after!' she said.

When Mrs Pinkerton-Trunks had wheeled Billie up the hill, she stopped under the shady tree, and took her shawl from her big handbag. Then she wrapped it tightly round Billie.

'I'm too hot!' said Billie.

'Babies don't talk, dear,' said Mrs Pinkerton-Trunks. 'In fact, tiny babies *can't* talk.'

'I'm not pretending to be a baby any more,' said Billie. But Mrs Pinkerton-Trunks just tumbled Billie out on to the grass.

'Time for a little snooze, dear!' she cried. 'Isn't this a *lovely* game?'

'NO!' cried Billie. 'I'm tired of being a baby.'

Mrs Pinkerton-Trunks took off her red hat, and fanned it back and forth to make a cooling breeze. As she fanned she sang a lullaby. 'Rock-a-bye, Billie, under the trees . . . . '

Billie lay on the grass, and looked up into the branches of the tree; the leaves were moving slightly, and between them, Billie could see the sky, and bright patches of sunlight. She tried to think of the time when she had been a real baby, and had lain in her pram – but no matter how hard she thought, she couldn't remember being a baby.

'I don't think I ever *was* a baby!' she said crossly.

'Nonsense, dear,' said Mrs Pinkerton-Trunks. 'Everyone was a baby, once.'

'Well – I'm not a baby *now*!' said Billie, and she struggled in the shawl until she stood upright on the grass. 'I'm going to play with Woodley!' she said, and she stamped off down the hill.

'Come back!' said Mrs Pinkerton-Trunks, 'Babies can't walk off like that!'

Billie hid in the bush. Then she saw Monkey go by, carrying his little blue watering can. 'Monkey!' she called. 'Would you like to play a game?'

'Yes, please!' said Monkey, and he came to join her in the bush.

Billie took off the shawl, and looked hard at Monkey. 'Monkey,' she said, 'would you like to pretend to be a tiny baby?' and before he could answer, she wrapped the shawl round him. Then she came out of the bush, and sat him on the edge of the path. 'Mrs Pinkerton-Trunks,' she called, 'here is a new baby for you!'

'Gurgle, gurgle!' said Monkey.

Billie and Mr Milford-Haven sat on the top of the hill, and watched as Mrs Pinkerton-Trunks wheeled Monkey round and round the path. 'I don't think babies play with watering cans, dear,' she said, and she took his little can from him, and put it down on the grass.

'Waah!' said Monkey.

'Little babies can't do a lot, can they?' said Billie to Mr Milford-Haven.

'No,' said Mr Milford-Haven. 'Neither can tiny lion cubs.'

'Come on, let's dance!'

And the three of them went off over the hill. Rum-tum-tiddle-I-rum-tum-tum . . . .

Billie Alone

Billie climbed up Mr Milford-Haven's tree, and sat down on a low branch. It was a wonderful place to be. She could see the pond, the bench, the shed, and the roof of Woodley's kennel. Woodley was running up and down the path, shouting, 'Come along! Where are you all?'

Billie watched Mr Milford-Haven, Monkey and Mrs Pinkerton-Trunks hurrying from the house. 'Here we are!' they called. 'Shall we set off straight away? What fun it will be!' They trotted off along the path, and were soon out of sight.

'I wonder where they are going?' said Billie to herself. But she didn't want to come down from the tree. It was lovely to be alone!

21

'I am all by myself,' said Billie. 'I am sitting in a tree – on my own.'

She leant against the trunk, and made up a song.

It was a happy song, and the words were very easy. They just said:

In a tree, on my own,
In the garden, on my own,
In a tree,
In a garden,
In the world.

Billie decided that when the animals came back she would sing her song to them – and then she fell asleep.

When she woke up, the sun was hidden behind a cloud, and everything was very still, and quiet.

'Woodley!' shouted Billie. 'Monkey!' But no one answered. Billie jumped down from the tree.

'Mr Milford-Haven!' she called. 'Mrs Pinkerton-Trunks!' But still no one called back to her. No friendly face came towards her through the long grass, and no one came out from behind a tree to say, 'Here I am!'

Billie went down the hill, and walked along the path. She looked into Woodley's kennel, but

Woodley wasn't there. She went to look on the garden bench, but there was no one sitting on it. She went to the shed, but she couldn't see the animals. There were only rows of plant pots standing on the shelves, and the garden tools propped in a corner.

'Monkey?' said Billie, hoping that he would pop up from behind a plant pot. But Monkey was nowhere to be seen.

Billie left the shed, and went down the path. 'I'm all alone,' she said quietly to herself. Then she shouted as loudly as she could, 'Animals! I am all alone!' But there was no answer.

Billie walked round and round the garden. She began to sing, to cheer herself up – but something strange had happened to her song. It wasn't happy any more. It was a sad song now. 'All alone, in the garden,' sang Billie, as she climbed the hill. She felt very sad and lonely, but when she was halfway up the hill she heard, from far away, the sound of a different song. A bright and happy song! '*Oooohh!*' it went,

The bear went over the mountain,
The bear went over the mountain,
The bear went over the mountain.

As Billie watched, the tip of Mrs Pinkerton-Trunks's trunk appeared over the top of the hill.

Then her red hat came into view, and Mr Milford-Haven's golden mane, Woodley's black patch, and Monkey's little brown head.

'*Oh!*' sang the animals, as they marched over the hill,

> '*The bear went over the mountain*
> *To see what he could see!*

Billie ran to meet them. She was singing a new song:

> '*Sometimes, I like to be alone,*
> *But I love to see my friends.*

The Picnic

One day, Billie went out to the garden with the animals, to have a picnic. They put the picnic food in the wagon, with the cups and plates, and the knife to cut the cake.

'Where shall we sit?' asked Billie.

'Let's sit on the top of the hill,' said Mrs Pinkerton-Trunks.

So everyone climbed the hill, and spread out the cloth, and got out the sandwiches. But no sooner had they begun to eat, than the wind began to blow. It blew the corners of the cloth over the food, and it blew the lettuce off Mr Milford-Haven's sandwich.

The animals sat one on each corner of the

cloth. 'But what's the use of a picnic if you can't move?' asked Woodley. And then he began to move very quickly indeed, scratching first with his front paw, and then with his back paw. Then everyone else began to scratch.

'We're sitting on an ants'-nest,' said Mr Milford-Haven. 'I think we'd better find another place!'

They put the food back into the wagon, folded the cloth, and set off, as quickly as they could.

'I think the side of the hill would be the best place,' said Woodley. 'We'll be sheltered from the wind, and we can see the pond, and the trees.'

Everyone thought that this was the best idea, and so they went half-way down the hill, spread the cloth, and took the food from the wagon again.

When they had eaten the sandwiches, they knocked the hard-boiled eggs against a stone and took off the shells. Monkey wanted to do his all by himself – but when his egg was out of the shell, he held it too tightly, and it popped up between his finger and thumb, and rolled down the hill.

Monkey jumped up and ran after his egg; and Billie ran after Monkey, to make sure that he didn't go near the water. But the egg rolled too quickly to be caught. It rolled into the pond – PLOP – and lay there like a great pearl amongst the pebbles and the stones. Billie and Monkey went back up the hill, and Billie gave him another egg.

When the eggs had been eaten, everyone was too full to eat any cake, so they left it to be eaten later. They lay on their backs, and looked at the clouds.

'Here's a cloud that looks like a castle,' said Mr Milford-Haven.

'Here's one that looks like a big beautiful white hat,' said Mrs Pinkerton-Trunks.

'Here's one that looks like a big black hat,' said Woodley – and it began to rain.

Billie put up the umbrella, and then turned the wagon upside-down and put it carefully over the cake, to keep it dry. Then everyone crowded close to Billie to shelter. Monkey became very worried about the cake, and after a moment or two, he scampered to the wagon, and sat underneath it, secretly picking off bits of icing, and one, two, three of the little red cherries.

Billie and the animals sat and watched the rain drip from the umbrella – first in drops – then in needles – and then so hard that the wagon couldn't be seen.

Then the rain stopped, and the sun came out.

Billie put down the umbrella, and everyone sat on the little patch of dry grass. Then she brought the cake from beneath the wagon, and cut it into five pieces. As she cut the fifth piece, Mrs Pinkerton-Trunks cried, 'Look, dear! A rainbow!' and everyone gazed up at the bands of colour which arched over the hill. Then, slowly, the colours faded.

'Where has it gone?' cried Monkey, running in little circles, and looking up at the sky. 'Where's the rainbow gone?'

'Vanished into the air,' said Woodley. 'Just disappeared.'

'Rather like the cherries on this cake, eh, Monkey?' said Mr Milford-Haven.

'Burp,' said Monkey. 'Burp.'

Where is
Mrs Pinkerton-Trunks?

Billie and the animals went for a walk in the woods. Deeper and deeper they went, until they reached a place where they had never been before. It was very exciting to find a new place – but it was also a bit frightening. They were so deep in the wood that they couldn't see the house, or the garden fence. Not even the path could be seen between the trunks of the trees.

'We are explorers,' said Woodley. 'That is, we have found this new place.' Billie could tell that he didn't really like being where he was.

'Well, now that we've found it, I think we should go home,' said Mrs Pinkerton-Trunks, and everyone agreed that this was the thing to do. They turned at once, and began to make their way back to the garden. As they went, they talked to one another. There was Woodley's bark, and Monkey's chatter, and Mr Milford-Haven's deep purr, all mixed up together into one friendly sound.

And then, quite suddenly, everyone stopped. Where was Mrs Pinkerton-Trunks? Billie and the animals looked around, but she was nowhere to be seen.

They called, 'Where are you?' but Mrs Pinkerton-Trunks didn't answer. They looked for her until the sky grew dark, and at last they began the journey home.

They walked slowly, each of them feeling very sad, and when they reached the garden gate, they turned and gazed at the dark wood.

It was dreadful to think of Mrs Pinkerton-Trunks alone in that mysterious place without a friendly face to smile at her.

'I feel very sad,' said Billie.

'My tail won't wag,' said Woodley, as they went into the warm, bright kitchen. 'I always wag my tail when I come home – but tonight, it just won't wag.'

Monkey looked at the wagon where Mrs Pinkerton-Trunks's shawl lay neatly folded in a corner. He sat on the rug, and put the shawl on his knee, and stroked it. His tea-time banana lay uneaten by his side. 'I feel too sad to eat it,' he said.

'We must try and think of something happy,' said Mr Milford-Haven. But no one could think of anything else but the dark wood, where Mrs Pinkerton-Trunks wandered, alone. One by one, they climbed the stairs, and huddled together in Billie's bed. One by one, they fell asleep.

When Billie woke it was early morning. The sun was shining through her window and, just for a moment, she felt happy. Then she re-membered that Mrs Pinkerton-Trunks was lost in the wood, and the sad feeling came back.

She got out of bed, and went to where Woodley sat by the window. He swished his tail across the floor to greet her.

'It still won't wag,' he said.

Billie sat on the window seat, and looked out at the garden, and the wood. 'Oh, Mrs Pinkerton-Trunks,' she said, 'please come back!' Then she leant her cheek against the window frame, and cried until her tears ran down the pane, like raindrops on a rainy day. Behind her, in the warm bed, Monkey curled into a little ball, and whimpered. Mr Milford-Haven patted his head and murmured, 'There, there, there.'

Woodley jumped up to sit beside Billie. Then, suddenly, he began to bark. His tail began to wag. Thump-thump-thump it went on the wooden seat. 'Mrs Pinkerton-Trunks!' he barked, for there she was, standing on the path, in the sunshine, smiling and waving her trunk.

'Yoohoo!' she called. 'It's me, my dears! Safe and happy, and home again!'

When they heard Mrs Pinkerton-Trunks's voice their sadness vanished. It was gone – POP! – as quickly and completely as a burst bubble!

Billie's Bad Dream

One night, Billie had a bad dream, and she woke up feeling frightened and alone. 'Daddy! Daddy!' she called, and was glad when her father opened the door.

'Everything's all right,' he said. 'You've had a bad dream, that's all.'

He drew back the curtains, so that she could see the moonlight, and then he went downstairs and brought back all the animals, to keep her company.

'Goodnight – pleasant dreams,' he said as he quietly closed the door.

The animals made themselves comfortable on Billie's bed. Woodley turned himself round three times, and then went straight to sleep. Monkey lay on Billie's pillow. Mr Milford-Haven stretched himself out at the end of the bed, and Mrs Pinkerton-Trunks sat by Billie's feet. She took her knitting from her bag, and began to knit. Click-click-click, went the needles. It was a comforting sound to hear.

'I once had a delightful dream, dear,' she said. 'I dreamed I bought the most beautiful hat. It was all covered with roses!'

Mr Milford-Haven opened an eye, and looked at her. 'I'm trying to go to sleep,' he said. 'I'm very tired. How can I go to sleep if you keep talking about hats?' He turned over and began to snore. Zzzzzzzzzzzzz!

'Yip-yip,' said Woodley, softly in his sleep. He wagged his tail, and his paws made little running movements. 'Woodley's having a nice dream,' said Monkey. 'He's dreaming that he's in the garden, chasing a ball.'

Swish-swish, went Woodley's tail. It knocked the ball of wool to the floor, and under the bed.

'I'll get it!' said Monkey. He jumped down to the rug, and stood there for a moment, yawning and rubbing his eyes. Then he disappeared under the bed. When he didn't come back, Mrs Pinkerton-Trunks went to look for him. She found him lying fast asleep, with his head on

Billie's slippers. It seemed such a pity to wake him that Mrs Pinkerton-Trunks lay down beside him, and curled her trunk around his shoulders to keep him warm.

Billie was beginning to feel drowsy. Her eyelids felt heavy. Little by little they were closing, although she tried hard to keep them open.

'Suppose the bad dream comes back?' she said.

Woodley opened his eyes and looked at her. 'A dream isn't real,' he said, 'even when it's a bad dream. And I am here, to keep you company . . . all . . . through . . . the night.'

He fell asleep again, and in his sleep he turned, and lay over Billie's feet. It was a warm, comforting feeling.

Billie looked at the sleeping animals. Each one slept in their own way. Woodley was curled into a ball. Mr Milford-Haven lay with his nose buried in his paws. Monkey slept with his thumb in his mouth, and Mrs Pinkerton-Trunks smiled in her sleep. The room was full of the sound of their breathing.

Billie lay back on her pillow and went to sleep. She dreamed that she was on a boat, rocking gently over the water. Mrs Pinkerton-Trunks sat by the sail, wearing a beautiful big hat, which was covered with roses. Woodley sat with

Monkey in the middle, and Mr Milford-Haven was at the back steering with his paw.

It was a lovely dream. Shush-shush-shush said the waves, and the little dream-ship sailed on until morning.

The Thing on Woodley's Nose

One sunny afternoon, Billie fell asleep in the garden. When she woke up, she found Woodley's face close to her own – and he looked so strange and funny that she thought that she must have been dreaming. His eyes were crossed, and his nose was twitching very gently. Twitch . . . twitch . . . twitch.

'Woodley,' whispered Billie, 'what are you doing?'

'There's something on my nose,' Woodley whispered back. 'I was sniffing in the grass, and a little black creature walked on my nose.'

Billie knelt, and looked closely at Woodley's face.

'I can't see anything,' she said.

'It's still there,' said Woodley, 'I can feel it. It tickles.'

'Why don't you just blow it off?' asked Billie.

'I don't want to do that,' said Woodley. 'It's a nice little creature, and I might blow it too far away from its family.'

Billie lay in the grass, and began to look for the family of the little black creature. She found a shining black beetle, and held it up on the palm of her hand.

'Here's a beetle!' she said.

Woodley sighed. 'That's nothing like the creature on my nose,' he said. 'It's much too big.'

Billie put the beetle on the grass, and watched as it hurried away.

In a little while Mr Milford-Haven came up the hill, and sat down beside Billie and Woodley. At first he didn't say anything. Then he coughed gently and said, 'Ahhemm! Why are you staring at Woodley's face?'

'There's a little black creature on it,' said Billie.

'And it tickles,' said Woodley.

'Why don't you just blow it away?' asked Mr Milford-Haven.

'I might blow it too far away from its brothers and sisters,' said Woodley.

Mr Milford-Haven bent and looked in the long grass. Then he raised his head. 'Is this the creature you're looking for?' he said.

Billie began to giggle. Mr Milford-Haven's eyes were crossed and there on his twitching nose was a red-spotted ladybird.

'No,' said Woodley. 'If my creature had spots on it, I would see them, wouldn't I?'

When Mrs Pinkerton-Trunks and Monkey came up the hill, they were surprised to see Woodley and Mr Milford-Haven sitting very still in the grass, with both their noses twitching gently.

'There's an ant on your nose,' said Monkey, 'just there!' and he touched Woodley's nose with a blade of grass.

'ATISHOOOO!' said Woodley.

Everyone lay down in the grass, to see what had happened to Woodley's ant. They found him almost at once – and hundreds more just like him; hundreds of black ants, all walking together, like an enormous family on a day's outing. Billie and the animals watched as they made their way over the root of a tree and disappeared from sight.

'Where are they going?' asked Billie, 'And what are they doing?'

'I don't know,' said Woodley, 'but I hope my ant enjoys himself – whatever it is.'

'Ahem!' said Mr Milford-Haven. 'The little spotted creature seems to have settled down on *my* nose.'

Billie turned, and put her arms around Mr Milford-Haven's neck. 'Ladybird, ladybird, fly away home,' she said, and the little ladybird spread her wings and flew away.

'Thank goodness for that,' said Mr Milford-Haven. 'They really do tickle, you know.'

Mrs Pinkerton-Trunks
and the Rose Garden

One day, Mrs Pinkerton-Trunks said to Billie, 'Do you know what I would like most in all the world, dear? A little rose garden!'

Billie was surprised. Mrs Pinkerton-Trunks had never talked about a rose garden before. 'Why do you want a rose garden?' she asked.

'It would be such a lovely thing to have,' said Mrs Pinkerton-Trunks. 'If I were feeling sad, I could go and sit there quietly, and smell the scent of the flowers.'

Billie went into the house, and put her arms around her father's neck. 'Mrs Pinkerton-Trunks wants a rose garden,' she whispered in his ear.

'It's very kind of you to want to help,' said

Billie's dad. 'Let's see what we can do.' He took Billie to the garden shed, and they found three little rose bushes. 'Do you think Mrs Pinkerton-Trunks would like these?'

'Oh, yes!' said Billie, and she ran to the top of the hill to show them to Mrs Pinkerton-Trunks.

Mrs Pinkerton-Trunks was very happy when she saw the rose bushes. Billie got her spade, then she and Mrs Pinkerton-Trunks climbed through the gap in the hedge, to look for a place which would be just right for the new garden.

They found a sunny spot, which was sheltered from the wind, and Billie began to dig. When she had turned over a patch of earth, Mrs Pinkerton-Trunks planted the first rose bush. As she patted the earth round the roots, she saw that the bush had a little white label tied to its stem.

Mrs Pinkerton-Trunks took her spectacles from her bag, and put them on. She peered at the label. 'The rose has a name!' she cried. 'It's called "Dorothy Perkins"!'

She looked at the labels on the other rose bushes, and read their names aloud to Billie, ' "Edna Harkness" and "Uncle Walter",' she said, 'two ladies and a gentleman. What a wonderful garden it will be!'

Billie and Mrs Pinkerton-Trunks worked hard, digging and planting the roses, until lunchtime.

For the rest of the Day, Mrs Pinkerton-Trunks talked about the roses called 'Edna Harkness', 'Dorothy Perkins' and 'Uncle Walter'. Monkey couldn't wait to see them. He slipped away, and climbed through the gap in the hedge. He was disappointed to find three bare twigs standing without a leaf or a flower. He stood for a while, and wondered which one was 'Uncle Walter'; then he climbed back through the gap, and went to find Billie.

'There are no roses in Mrs Pinkerton-Trunks's garden!' he said.

'The roses haven't grown yet,' said Billie.

The next morning, Monkey woke very early, and ran down to the gap in the hedge to see if the roses had grown yet. But the bushes were still bare. Monkey saw their brown branches poking up through the morning mist. He waited until the sun came up, but even when the mist vanished, there wasn't one rose to be seen. There was nothing but three little naked bushes standing in the earth, with their names tied to their stems.

'Please, Dorothy Perkins,' said Monkey, 'please, Edna Harkness, hurry up and grow. Mrs Pinkerton-Trunks will be here soon!'

Billie and the animals had their breakfast, and wondered where Monkey was. They searched the house for him, but he was nowhere to be seen. 'Monkey!' they called as they climbed the hill, but he didn't answer.

Billie and Mrs Pinkerton-Trunks went down to the bottom of the garden, and as they came to the gap in the hedge, they heard a little voice say, 'Please grow, Dorothy Perkins!'

'Oh, Monkey, dear,' said Mrs Pinkerton-Trunks, when they reached the new garden, 'roses don't grow in a day. It takes a long time – they need sunshine and rain, and someone to look after them.'

Monkey walked slowly back to the house to have his breakfast. Although he knew it would take a long time, he went to the garden every day to look for the roses. When the summer came, the roses bloomed – just as Mrs Pinkerton-Trunks said they would.

So, if you ever find a small and secret rose garden – it may belong to Mrs Pinkerton-Trunks. And the roses in it are called: Edna Harkness, Dorothy Perkins – and Uncle Walter.

Monkey Makes a House

One day in the garden, Billie set up her box house on the top of the hill. All the animals – except Money – pretended to be guests, and went to visit her. 'Knock, knock' on the door they went, and Billie opened it to each animal in turn and said, 'How do you do? Please come in.'

Monkey sat on the bench and watched them. 'I want to have a house of my own,' he said.

'You can use my kennel if you like,' said Woodley. 'I shan't be in it – I'm visiting Billie.'

Monkey went to look at Woodley's kennel. He walked all round it; then he went inside it; and then he came out again. 'Don't like it!' He went back to the bench, and sat down again, and put his arms across his chest and hugged himself. 'I wanted a little special house!' he shouted.

And then he noticed Mrs Pinkerton-Trunks's shawl lying in the grass. Monkey took it and held it up. It was too big for his little arms to hold it out straight, so he laid it down on the side of the hill. It was a pretty shawl, and all round the edges were little fluffy tassels.

'I'll make a tent,' said Monkey, 'a nice, lacey tent,' and he scampered round the hill, gathering up the shawl.

When Monkey had bundled up the shawl in his arms, he went back to the bench and began to make his tent. He hung the shawl over the back of the bench, and held the corners down with stones. Then he crept inside his tent-house, and sat down. It was lovely in his house, he thought; but after a while he began to think about the cushions that were in Billie's house.

'I could have just *one* cushion,' he thought, and he went out of his tent, and ran up the hill to the box house, where he snatched up a cushion. 'Monkey!' said Billie, and she ran out after him – but he was nowhere to be seen.

In his tent house, Monkey put the cushion on the ground and sat down on it. It was lovely and soft. But after a moment or two he thought, 'If I had *two* cushions, there would be a place for a guest to sit . . . .' And he ran back up the hill.

The box house was empty, as Billie and her guests had gone for a run round the hill. Monkey picked up the cushion . . . and then he took a curtain . . . and then he saw the pink tea-set with the blue flowers.

'If I had a tea-set,' Monkey told himself, 'I could have guests to tea, like Billie does . . . .' And in his imagination he saw how everyone would sit in the lacey tent, on soft cushions and rugs, and how he, Monkey, would pour the tea.

He balanced the tea-set on top of the cushion, as quickly as he could, for he could hear the voices of Billie and the animals as they came up the far side of the hill – then he staggered down the hill again towards his tent. As he passed the kennel he saw Woodley's drinking bowl. 'Flowers!' thought Monkey. 'I'll put flowers in a bowl in my house!'

When Billie and the animals saw the empty box house, they set off to look for the missing cushions, curtains, rug and tea-set. 'I'm afraid I can't find my shawl, either, dear,' said Mrs Pinkerton-Trunks.

'And my bowl's gone missing, too,' said Woodley, as they went by his kennel.

Then they saw the tent-house and, one by one, they went inside to see Monkey busily arranging daisies in Woodley's drinking bowl.

He was squatting on one of the cushions, and the sunlight, shining through the lacey shawl, dappled him all over with light and shadow.

Monkey looked up, and his eyes grew very big and round. 'I wanted to make a nice house, and ask you all to tea,' he said.

'Oh, Monkey!' said Billie. 'We all wondered where our things had gone. You should have *asked* to borrow them.'

Monkey gazed at her. 'Please may I borrow a cushion ... ?' he said. 'And some curtains ... and another cushion ... andarugandashawlandateaset, please?'

'Oh, *Monkey*,' said Billie, giggling, 'of course you can!'

'Thank you,' said Monkey.

Measles are Catching

One morning, Billie woke up with a running nose, streaming eyes, and an itchy feeling about the chest. Her father stood by her bed, looking down on her. 'It may be the measles,' he said, and he went to fetch the thermometer. But the thermometer didn't show that Billie was hotter than she should have been – or colder. Her father undid the buttons on her pyjamas, and peered at her chest. It looked just as it always looked.

He tucked the bed-clothes round her, and brought up the animals to keep her company, then went downstairs to telephone the doctor.

When her father had left the room Billie got

out of bed, and knelt on the landing, and peeped through the bannister railings. Below in the hall, she could hear her father dialling the number.

'What will happen to me if I get the measles?' she called.

'Not a lot,' said her father, 'a snuffle or two – a pink spot or two . . . now back to bed with you!'

Billie lay in her bed, and the animals sat in a circle round her, and waited for the spots to appear. But a whole five minutes went by, and there wasn't a spot to be seen.

'I don't think she's got the measles,' said Woodley, who sat on Billie's pillow, staring at her chest. 'She isn't at all spotted.'

'Never mind!' said Monkey, and he snuggled down beside Billie, and gave her a hug to cheer her up.

'But I don't want to be spotted!' said Billie.

'It might look rather nice, dear,' said Mrs Pinkerton-Trunks, 'lots of pretty little dots. It will make a nice change for you!'

By and by, Billie's father came into the room, with a glass of orange juice. 'I remember the day when *I* caught the measles!' he said.

'Caught them!' said Billie.

'Some illnesses are passed from person to person,' said her father. 'I give it to you; you give it to someone else; and there we are – all spotty together!' He smiled at her, as he went out of the room. 'Have a little sleep!' he said, and he quietly closed the door behind him.

Billie sat up in bed. 'Measles are *catching*!' she said, and she turned to the animals, but they were gone. Disappeared. Vanished into thin air. 'Animals!' she called. 'Where are you?'

'We thought we'd just sit up here for a while, dear,' said Mrs Pinkerton-Trunks. 'It's really quite an interesting place to sit. And the view is delightful!'

Billie looked up, and there they were, sitting in a row on the top of her wardrobe.

'It's not that we *mind* catching your measles,' said Mr Milford-Haven.

'It's just that we'd rather not,' said Woodley.

Billie lay back on her pillow, and sneezed. 'Bless you,' said a voice from beneath the bed-clothes.

'Monkey?' said Billie, and she lifted the sheet, and saw him sitting at the bottom of the bed, smiling and waving to her. Billie crept down to the end of the bed, and gave him a hug. Monkey put his arms round her, and hugged her in return.

It was cosy lying at the bottom of the bed, holding Monkey's warm little body, and before she knew it, Billie had fallen asleep.

She was awakened by Doctor Jones lifting the bed-clothes and smiling down on her. 'You haven't got the measles,' he said, 'just a cold in the head. Stay in bed today, and tomorrow you'll feel much better!'

'Well,' said Mr Milford-Haven when Doctor Jones had gone, 'that's what I've said all along. She hasn't got the measles – what she's got is a . . . a . . . a . . . TISHOOOOOO!

'Cuckoo!'

Billie and the animals hadn't been out to play in the garden for a long time, because every day a cold wind blew ... every day it rained and rained ... every day the sky was full of dark clouds. Nothing was fun any more.

Monkey was so cold that he wore his blue blanket like a shawl. It covered his head, and it was pinned under his chin with a brooch which belonged to Mrs Pinkerton-Trunks. He didn't look like Monkey at all, but like some strange blue animal – a sad, cold little animal.

One morning, when Monkey woke up, he looked through the kitchen window, and saw that the sky was blue. 'Ooooh!' he said, and he opened the door, and trotted off down the path. As he went, he heard a little voice, which said, 'Cuckoo!'

Monkey looked in a bush, but he couldn't see anything. 'Hello,' he said. 'Who's there?'

'Cuckoo!' said the little voice once more.

Monkey ran back to the house, to Billie and the animals. 'There's something in the garden saying "cuckoo"!' he said, excitedly. Then he turned, and ran back along the path, and up the hill, with his blue blanket floating out behind him.

Billie and the animals followed him to see who was making the strange sound. Mr Milford-Haven prowled round the bush. 'I say!' he called. 'What are you in there?'

'Cuckoo!' said the voice.

Mr Milford-Haven went into the bush. When he came out again, he was smiling. 'There's nothing in there,' he said, 'but the bush is full of new, sticky buds.'

Billie and the animals went to look – and Mr Milford-Haven was right. The branches of the bush were full of little buds, all tightly wrapped, like little parcels. 'Inside the little parcels are the new leaves!' said Mr Milford-Haven.

Billie and the animals climbed further up the hill. When they reached the top, they found

Monkey dancing beneath three tall trees. 'Look at the daffodils!' he said.

Mr Milford-Haven bent down to smell the flowers. Sniff-sniff-sniff, he went. And as he sniffed, he closed his eyes. 'I feel very happy,' he said, 'I feel FULL OF FUN! I feel JOYFUL!'

To everyone's surprise, he got up and began to dance with Monkey. Round and round the hilltop they went, waving the blue blanket. Billie, Woodley and Mrs Pinkerton-Trunks sat down to watch them.

It was wonderful to sit on the new soft grass – and it was wonderful to watch Mr Milford-Haven dancing; for no one had ever seen him dance before.

'Bravo!' cried Mrs Pinkerton-Trunks.

'Cuckoo!' said the little voice.

Woodley jumped to his feet. He looked down a rabbit hole. He went to look inside his kennel, but he couldn't discover what was making the strange little sound.

'We must look everywhere until we find it,' said Billie. But Woodley wasn't listening to her. He was wagging his tail: swish-swish. And Mrs Pinkerton-Trunks was humming a tune. 'Hmm-hmm!' she sang. And then she sang aloud, 'Tra-la!' and got up and joined the dance.

Woodley looked at Billie. 'Come on,' he said. 'Let's dance!'

Billie got up. 'Woodley,' she said, 'I'm not dressed yet. I forgot to get dressed!'

'Well, dance in your pyjamas,' said Woodley.

So, Billie danced in her pyjamas. She danced until she was out of breath, then she lay on her back, and looked up at the blue sky. The animals came and sat by her side. Mrs Pinkerton-Trunks straightened her hat on her head. Monkey folded his blanket. Woodley shook himself, and Mr Milford-Haven gazed dreamily at the pond. The garden was still and quiet, except for the little sound – 'Cuckoo!'

Billie and the animals made their way down the hill. As they went, they listened for the sound of the little voice. 'I think it's gone forever,' said Monkey – but just as they reached the kitchen door, it came again, just once more. 'Cuckoo!' it said.

It was such a happy sound that everyone smiled. Then they rushed into the kitchen, hungry for breakfast – full of the joys of spring!

The Letter

One morning, Billie got a letter – it was propped up by her blue cereal bowl when she came down for breakfast. It was in a white envelope, and it had a stamp, and a black, wavey post-mark. Billie opened her letter and her father read it for her. The letter was from her auntie, asking her to tea on Saturday.

When Billie had eaten her breakfast, she took the letter out into the garden to show it to the animals. 'It says, "Dear Billie," ' she said, ' "Will you come to tea on Saturday? We will have chocolate cake, and ice-cream. Your loving Auntie Pat. XXXXX." '

Woodley looked at Billie and sighed. 'I wish

someone would send me a loving letter asking me to tea . . . with chocolate cake.'

'I'll send you a letter,' said Billie.

'You can't write,' said Woodley. 'You couldn't write 'Chocolate cake'.

'I'll send you *this* letter!' said Billie, and she knocked on the side of his kennel and shouted. 'Post's come!'

Woodley was very pleased. He took his letter from the envelope, and said that it was from his brother Arthur. ' "Please come to tea!" That's what it says,' said Woodley.

But because Billie and Woodley had got a letter, all the other animals wanted one too. 'Send *me* a letter,' said Monkey, sitting on a branch of a tree. 'I want a letter too!'

So Mrs Pinkerton-Trunks lifted the letter in her trunk, and gave it to Monkey. He opened it and read it where he sat. ' "Dear Monkey," ' he said, ' "Please come to tea! We will have *two* chocolate cakes, and ice cream. Your loving Grandpa. XXXXXXX" '

Then it was Mr Milford-Haven's turn to get the letter, and he went to the top of the hill to wait for the postman. Billie and Woodley climbed after him. When they reached the top, they dropped the letter in the grass and shouted, 'Post's come!'

Mr Milford-Haven opened his letter and

began to read. 'Good Heavens!' he said, 'What a surprise! Six chocolate cakes! Well, well, well . . . !'

When he had finished reading the letter, he put it back in the envelope.

'Who is your letter from?' asked Billie.

'It's confidential,' said Mr Milford-Haven.

'He means it's a secret,' explained Woodley as he and Billie went to deliver the letter to Mrs Pinkerton-Trunks.

Mrs Pinkerton-Trunks was very pleased to get a letter. She rummaged about in her bag for her spectacles. Then she opened her letter and began to read.

'It's from my cousin!' she said. 'It says, "Dear Old Pinkers! Will you come to tea? We will have *ten* large chocolate cakes, and vanilla ice-cream. After tea we will have a walk in the park, and listen to the band. Stay the night if you can! Bring your toothbrush, and your pyjamas!" '

'Mrs Pinkerton-Trunks!' said Billie. 'The letter doesn't say all that!'

'Yes it does, dear,' said Mrs Pinkerton-Trunks. 'My cousin always writes a long letter.'

It was almost time for lunch, and Billie and the animals went into the house. From the kitchen window they could see Mrs Pinkerton-Trunks on the top of the hill, still reading the letter.

Billie ran back up the hill. 'Mrs Pinkerton-Trunks,' she said. 'It can't take such a long time to read your letter!'

'Well, dear,' said Mrs Pinkerton-Trunks, taking off her spectacles, and putting them back in her bag, 'it wasn't the letter itself that took such a time to read – it was all the kisses at the bottom!'

Mrs Pinkerton-Trunks
to the Rescue

One cold winter's day, Billie and the animals were walking in the garden when a gust of wind blew Mrs Pinkerton-Trunks's hat up into the air. I blew across the frozen pond, and landed – PLOP! – in the middle of the ice.

Billie crouched by the edge of the pond and stretched out her hand. But the hat was too far away for her to reach. Woodley couldn't reach it. Mr Milford-Haven couldn't reach it. Even Mrs Pinkerton-Trunks's long trunk couldn't stretch so far across the pond.

'I'll get it! I'll get it!' said Monkey, and before

anyone could stop him, he ran across the ice, picked up the hat, and put in on his head.

'Be careful!' called Billie.

'Watch out!' barked Woodley.

'Come back at once!' called Mrs Pinkerton-Trunks. 'You'll have a nasty accident!'

But Monkey just giggled and said, 'Look! I'm skating! I'm skating on the pond!'

Billie and the animals watched and held their breath as Monkey skated back and forth across the ice. He whirled! He twirled! And then, quite suddenly, he stopped. The ice was beginning to crack beneath his feet. One long crack ran away from beneath his left foot. A long crack appeared beneath his right foot – and then a lot of little cracks appeared, one after the other – crack-crack-crack-crack-crack!

Monkey began to run. As he ran, the long cracks in the ice seemed to run behind him. He looked over his shoulder as he went, and saw them catching up with him. 'Hurry! Hurry!' called Billie and the animals.

Monkey ran towards the edge of the pond. As he ran, he saw Billie holding out her arms, and Mrs Pinkerton-Trunks stretching out her trunk, to catch him and snatch him from the ice.

'Just a little further, dear!' she shouted – but it was too late. C-R-A-C-K! The ice broke up, and Monkey fell – SPLASH – into the cold water.

It was very frightening to go down into the icy water, and when Monkey bobbed up again, he was very glad to see Mrs Pinkerton-Trunks leaning out carefully over the pond. Mr Milford-Haven and Woodley were holding on to her tail.

Slowly . . . slowly . . . her trunk came nearer, until at last it wrapped itself round Monkey, and he was pulled back on to the land. Mrs Pinkerton-Trunks wrapped him in her shawl.

'I'm glad you're an elephant,' said Monkey, shivering and dripping. 'If you weren't an elephant, you wouldn't have a trunk . . . and I would still be in the water!'

A Hat for Woodley

One cold windy day, Billie and Woodley went for a walk in the garden. It was so windy that Woodley's ears were blown straight back; and when he and Billie turned the bend in the path, the wind blew his ears straight forwards.

'Right!' said Woodley, and he marched to the top of the hill – where the wind blew his ears across his face.

'Oh . . . Woodley . . . !' giggled Billie, and she crouched in front of him and held up his ears so that he could see.

'What I need is a dog-hat,' he said.

'Oh . . . Woodley,' said Billie. 'There's no such thing!'

'Yes, there is,' said Woodley. 'I have just invented it.'

He got up, and ran down the hill. When Billie followed him, she found him in the kitchen, putting on Mrs Pinkerton-Trunks's red hat and looking at himself in the mirror. 'This isn't a good dog-hat,' he said. 'It doesn't cover my ears! I want something bigger.'

'I'll find you a hat!' said Monkey, and he ran to the table and took the blue tea-cosy from the tea-pot. Woodley put it on. It covered his ears – but it covered his eyes as well.

'Oh, Woodley,' said Billie. 'You can't wear a tea-cosy! You won't be able to see where you're going!'

'Yes, I will!' said Woodley. 'Dogs can find their way by their sense of smell.' And he marched from the kitchen and straight into a bush.

Billie and Monkey ran after him, and lifted the tea-cosy from his head. Woodley sighed. 'There must be a hat *somewhere* that would stop a dog's ears from flapping,' he said.

'I'll find a hat for you!' said Billie, and she went into the house with Monkey and gathered together three hats: a pink paper party hat, a yellow dressing-up hat, and a white baby-bonnet. Mrs Pinkerton-Trunks and Mr Milford-Haven helped carry them to the bush.

'Ha-ha-ha!' said Mr Milford-Haven as Woodley

tried on the yellow hat. 'Dashed amusing. I do beg your pardon, but you look so funny.'

'Looks aren't everything, dear!' said Mrs Pinkerton-Trunks, as she put the pink paper party hat on Woodley's head. Then she gave such a loud snort of laughter that the hat was blown straight off again.

'Thank you so much!' said Woodley, as he watched the paper hat drift through a gap in the bush.

He picked up the baby-bonnet, and Billie put it on for him, tying the ribbons under his chin. He looked so funny that Monkey stuffed his fingers in his mouth to keep himself from laughing.

'RIGHT!' said Woodley, and he strode from the bush, and disappeared down the path.

And as soon as Woodley was out of sight, everyone let out their laughter in one great rush of sound. They laughed so much that the bush shook with the noise, but when at last the laughter died down, there could still be heard, from afar, the sound of giggles and hiccups. And when Billie and the animals went down the path, they found Woodley shaking with laughter, and gazing at his reflection in his shiny drinking bowl.

'Ooh!' he gasped, 'I've never . . . HIC . . . seen . . . never . . . so HIC HIC . . . never . . . !' He rolled over on the grass, and Billie watched him in amazement.

Then Mr Milford-Haven began to laugh too. 'Ha-ha!' he said. 'I do believe he's laughing at himself. I do believe he's seen the funny side of this at last!'

How Many Daisies?

One day, Billie wanted to know how tall she was, so her father stood her against the wall, and made a pencil mark just above her head. The mark was right next to a daisy on the wallpaper.

Then Billie's father counted them for her, starting with the daisy nearest to the floor, and going higher, and higher, and higher.

When Billie's father had gone out into the garden, the animals came to look at the mark. One by one, they stood by the wall, and Billie made a mark at the top of their heads. First there was Mrs Pinkerton-Trunks's mark, eight daisies high; and then Mr Milford-Haven's, six daisies high; then Woodley's, four daisies and, last of all, Monkey's. Monkey's mark was so close to the ground that Billie had to kneel down to make it.

Monkey wasn't very pleased. 'I'm taller than that!' he said.

'No, you're not,' said Billie, and she counted the daisies – one, two.

Monkey sighed, and *he* counted them – one, two. 'Please measure me again?' he said to Mrs Pinkerton-Trunks.

Mrs Pinkerton-Trunks took a length of wool and held one end against the top of Monkey's head. The other end just reached his toes. 'There!' said Mrs Pinkerton-Trunks. 'That's how tall you are.'

Monkey took the piece of wool, and looked at it. It wasn't very long, he thought. In fact, it was quite short.

For the rest of the day Monkey carried his piece of wool about with him, and from time to time he looked at it, and thought, 'I wish I was taller than that.' When night-time came he lay in the wagon, and stared at the marks on the wall. He stared . . . and he stared . . . and he wished . . . and he wished.

Upstairs, Billie lay asleep in her bed. She was awakened by the sound of something heavy being dragged across the kitchen floor. She went downstairs, and opened the door. Monkey was standing on a chair close to the kitchen wall. He was holding a crayon in his hand, making a big blue dot just above his head, next to the sixth daisy from the floor.

'Oh, Monkey, that's cheating . . . ,' said Billie. 'It doesn't matter to me how tall you are.'

Monkey jumped down to the floor. 'But I'm only two daisies tall,' he sobbed.

Then Billie saw the teacloth on the back of the chair.

'Look,' she said, 'I know you're only two daisies tall, but on the teacloth you measure six squares.'

Monkey wiped away his tears and smiled proudly at Billie.

Pretending

One day, when Billie and the animals were in the garden, they were surprised to see Monkey come bounding along the path.

'I'm pretending to be a kangeroo!' he said as he went by. 'Isn't it good?'

But when he came round the hill again he stopped by the bench. 'I haven't got a pouch,' he said. 'All kangeroos have a pouch. A sort of pocket thing in the front.'

'Never mind, dear,' said Mrs Pinkerton-Trunks, and she hung her handbag round his neck. 'Pretend that my bag is your pouch!'

Monkey was very pleased, and off he went

again. Billie and the animals sat on the bench and waited for him to reappear, but when he came round the hill again, Mrs Pinkerton-Trunks's bag was hanging from his shoulder. 'I'm pretending to be the conductor of a bus!' he said. 'Tickets please! Hold very tight please! Ding-ding!'

'I'll pretend to be the driver!' said Woodley.

'And I'll pretend to be a passenger!' said Mrs Pinkerton-Trunks.

Billie watched as the bus made its way round the hill, then she turned to Mr Milford-Haven. 'Shall *we* pretend to be something?' she asked.

'Good idea!' said Mr Milford-Haven. 'I shall pretend to be a lion, lying on a bench.'

'But Mr Milford-Haven,' said Billie, 'you *are* a lion lying on a bench! You've got to pretend to be something else.'

'Ah . . . !' said Mr Milford-Haven. 'I see what you mean. Very well, I shall be a . . . a . . . what are *you* going to be?'

'A cat!' said Billie. 'Look!' She curled up in the grass, and made a purring noise. Then she stretched and yawned, and said, 'Miaoooow!'

'That's jolly good!' said Mr Milford-Haven. 'Look what I'm pretending to be!' He began to run along the path, by the flower-beds, stopping from time to time to put the tip of his nose in a flower. 'Bzzzzzz!' he said.

'You're a bee!' said Billie. 'You're pretending to be a bee!'

'That's right!' said Mr Milford-Haven. 'You've guessed!'

And then he stopped buzzing and looked at Billie. 'Aren't I rather on the large side for a bee?' he asked. He looked so disappointed that Billie sat down beside him and gave him a hug. 'When you're pretending it doesn't matter *what* size you are!' she said, 'Just *pretend* that you're small!'

So Mr Milford-Haven closed his eyes, and pretended that he was small. Then up he got, and off he went, whizzing down the hill – bzzzzzz – and back again – bzzzzzz – and along the path – bzzzzzz – and round the pond – bzzzzzz.

Billie sat on the top of the hill, and watched as Woodley drove the bus to the trees. Everyone got out, and lay in the grass, and listened to the sound of the wind in the leaves.

'It sounds like the sea,' said Billie. 'Shall we pretend that we are on a ship, sailing over the ocean?'

They climbed on to the low branch of Mr Milford-Haven's tree, and imagined that they were bobbing up and down on the blue waves of the sea. Woodley made the sound of the ship's bell, Billie and Mrs Pinkerton-Trunks made the sound of the sea, and Monkey made the sound of the wind.

They *closed their eyes* as they made the sounds, and it was as if they really were at sea, with the land far, far away.

Then suddenly, they heard a strange noise. 'Bzzzz,' it went. 'Bzzzzz.'

'Buzz?' said Woodley, and everyone opened their eyes to see Mr Milford-Haven climbing on to the branch. 'I'm a bee!' he said happily.

'But we're pretending to be on a ship!' said Billie.

'Ah ... !' said Mr Milford-Haven. 'In that case, I'll be a sea-gull, shall I?' He drew in his breath, and gave a loud 'SQUAWK!' It startled everyone so much that they tumbled from the branch, and lay in the grass.

'I say!' said Mr Milford-Haven. 'Awfully sorry! Er ... could we all pretend to be swimming?'

And so they all swam home for tea.

The Jumble Sale

One day, Billie and her father decided that they would go to a jumble sale, and take some of Billie's old clothes. They went into the bedroom and opened the chest of drawers. Then they took out the things, one by one, and looked at them.

'Some of these things are too small for you,' said Billie's father. 'But they will fit someone else.'

They folded the clothes and put them into a cardboard box, and then they looked at the shoes. All Billie's shoes fitted her, except for a pair of red sandals which hurt her toes because they were too small.

Billie put the sandals in the box with the clothes, then she picked up her red wellingtons. There was a hole in one wellington which let in the water – and a wellington boot with a hole in it is no use to anyone. Billie took the red wellingtons, and put them in the dustbin.

Monkey went with her, and watched as the wellingtons were dropped into the dustbin. He was very excited about the jumble sale, and after tea he crept up the stairs, and hid in the box of T-shirts and dungarees. He had just snuggled down in a corner of the box, when he felt it being lifted into the air. Then it swayed back and forth, as Billie's father carried it down the stairs. It was just like being rocked in a cradle. It was such a nice feeling that Monkey fell asleep, and didn't wake up until he was in the hall where the jumble sale was being held.

It was very bright and noisy in the hall, and Monkey peeped over the side of the box and blinked in the light. All round him were stalls heaped with clothes, curtains, cushions, hats and handbags.

'Oooooo!' said Monkey, but before he could say anything else, his box was turned upside down, and he was dumped – FLUMP! – into a heap of blankets.

All round, people were buying things and Monkey was tossed about until he was breathless.

It was like a wonderful, exciting game, he thought; and he tumbled about until he reached the end of the stall, and lay giggling by the side of a cloth cat, who had no whiskers, and only one ear.

'Aren't jumble sales exciting!' Monkey said to the cat. 'I think they are the most—'

But before he could finish telling the cat what he thought, he heard a cry of 'MONKEY!' And there was Billie, standing before him, looking very surprised.

'I wanted to come to the jumble sale,' said Monkey.

'Oh, *Monkey*!' said Billie. 'Someone might have bought you, and taken you home! Everything is for sale, you see.' As she spoke, the woman behind the stall lifted Monkey by his leg and dangled him in front of Billie. 'Do you want to buy this monkey?' she asked. 'He only costs five pence.'

Billie looked at Monkey's little brown face, which hung before her, upside down. 'Oh – yes!' said Billie, and she counted out five pennies as quickly as she could.

'Five pennies!' said Monkey, as he sat on Billie's shoulder with his arms around her neck, 'A whole five pennies! You must love me an awful lot!'

'Yes,' said Billie. 'I do!'

Something Special

One day, Mr Milford-Haven went down to the pond to drink, and as he bent over the water, he saw his reflection: a lovely picture of himself, surrounded by reeds and bullrushes. There were his eyes, his nose, his ears, and his *mane*. He was very pleased and proud, and he turned and went back up the hill to where Billie and the animals were sitting.

'I've just seen myself in the pond,' he said. 'And do you know, I'm the only one amongst us who has a mane!'

'I don't think that you should look at yourself in the pond, dear,' said Mrs Pinkerton-Trunks. 'It's a dangerous thing to do – and anyway, the water wobbles, and you can't see yourself properly.' She reached into her handbag, and brought out a mirror, and held it so that Mr Milford-Haven could look at himself again.

'Magnificent, isn't it?' he said, and he shook his head so that his mane stood out in a great golden cloud. 'It's wonderful to have something as special as a mane!'

'Look what *I've* got!' said Monkey, getting rather excited and scrambling up a tree. 'A lovely long tail!' And he curled his tail round a low branch, and swung to and fro.

'Well, *I've* got a tail,' said Woodley, who lay with his nose on his paws, gazing up into the tree.

'So have I, dear,' said Mrs Pinkerton-Trunks.

'And *I* have,' said Mr Milford-Haven. 'We've all got tails, young Monkey.'

'No, we haven't,' said Billie. 'I haven't got a tail.'

'Ah . . . yes,' said Mr Milford-Haven. 'Forgot for a moment. Thought you were an animal, like us.'

'I've got a ta-a-ail!' shouted Monkey. 'I can swing from a branch!'

'Well, so can I!' said Billie, and she jumped up and clung to the branch. 'I've got fingers and thumbs!'

'So have I!' said Monkey, and he sat with Billie

on the branch, and they both wiggled their fingers.

'*I* seem to be the only one who hasn't got something that the others haven't got,' said Woodley, and he got up and marched down the hill, and disappeared into the bush.

Billie and Monkey jumped down from the tree, and everyone looked carefully at one another. Woodley was right – he hadn't got a trunk like an elephant; and he hadn't got a mane like a lion; and he hadn't got fingers and thumbs. Billie ran down to the bush, to try to make him feel better. 'You're the only one who can bark!' she said, looking at him through the leaves of the bush.

'That is something I *say*,' said Woodley. 'Woof-woof. Everyone has a voice. I wanted something special, like a trunk or a mane or fingers and thumbs.'

Billie crept into the bush, and sat beside him. 'You've got a lovely sort of waggy tail,' she said.

'So have Mrs Pinkerton-Trunks and Mr Milford-Haven,' said Woodley, 'not to mention Monkey . . . . '

'I haven't got a tail,' said Billie. 'I'm a person.'

'You've got fingers and thumbs,' said Woodley.

Billie sighed. She gazed at him in silence – and then . . . .

'Woodley,' she said.

'What?'

'You've got a lovely black patch on your back.'

Woodley pricked up his ears. 'Have I?' he said, and he ran from the bush, and up the hill to look at himself in Mrs Pinkerton-Trunks's mirror.

'Come and look at my patch!' he shouted. 'It's wonderful – it's very black! It's on my back!'

When the patch had been admired, Billie and Woodley went down the hill together. 'Woodley,' said Billie, as they went, 'even though the others have tails, there is something special about yours.'

'Is there?' said Woodley.

'Yes!' said Billie. 'You can show me how happy you are by wagging it!'

A Rainy Day

One day, Billie and the animals set out to go to the garden. 'It may rain,' Billie said, and so she took her red wellingtons, and her father's big, black umbrella.

Billie and the animals climbed the hill and when they reached the top, Woodley looked up at the sky.

'*I* think the sun will shine all day,' he said.

But as he spoke, the sun went behind a dark cloud.

' . . . or then again, it may not,' said Woodley.

'I say!' said Mr Milford-Haven. 'It's raining!'

Billie put up the big, black umbrella, and everyone sat beneath it and listened to the sounds of the rain. At first it went 'pit – pit'; then, 'pitpat – pitpat – pitpat'; then 'pitterpitter – pitterpitter'. Then it fell so hard that almost nothing could be seen of the garden.

And then it began to thunder and the lightning began to flash. Monkey shouted 'Hurrah!' and ran away over the wet grass.

'How can we get him back, without some of us getting wet?' asked Billie. 'If I take the umbrella, *you* will get wet, and if I leave the umbrella for you, *I* shall get wet.'

'Suppose we all go together?' said Mr Milford-Haven.

'What a good idea!' said Billie.

Although Billie and the animals kept as close together as they could, the umbrella wasn't quite big enough to cover them all.

'I'm afraid my mane is getting a bit soggy,' said Mr Milford-Haven.

'And my trunk is quite wet, dear,' said Mrs Pinkerton-Trunks.

'Your *trunk*!' said Woodley. 'What about my tail?'

'We need another umbrella,' said Billie.

'And a lot more wellington boots,' said Woodley.

'Allow me!' said Mr Milford-Haven, and he put his two front legs into Billie's wellington boots, and strode out over the wet grass. 'Help will soon be at hand!' he cried. 'I shall return with umbrellas and boots by the dozen!' Then his two front paws slid forwards, and he found himself lying on the grass.

Mr Milford-Haven sat up, took off the boots and gave them back to Billie. 'Tummy and Paws a bit damp!' he said.

'This is what you should have done,' said Woodley, and he put his two back legs into the boots. But the boots were too long for him, and after a few steps downhill, he found that he was almost upside down.

'I don't think that you should stand on your head in the rain, dear!' called Mrs Pinkerton-Trunks.

Woodley sighed, took off the boots, and gave them back to Billie.

Monkey crept quietly up behind them.

'Let me try!' he said. And before anyone could stop him, he leapt into one of the boots . . . and disappeared.

'Help!' he said. 'It's very dark in here . . . and I think I'm slipping.'

And so he was, going faster and faster down the hill. When the boot reached the bottom of the hill it stood upright for a moment, then it fell over with a thud.

'To the rescue!' cried Mr Milford-Haven, and he raced down the hill. But when he reached the boot, he found that Monkey was stuck in the toe. Woodley went to his aid, and shook the boot from side to side. Then Billie and Mrs Pinkerton-Trunks arrived, and Billie held the boot while the elephant put her long trunk inside, to bring out the little monkey.

When Monkey had been rescued from the boot, everyone went home.

'My goodness,' said Billie's father. 'You are all wet! Where's the umbrella?'

'On the top of the hill,' said Billie.

Kings and Queens

One day, Billie took an old crimson curtain and a shiny gold paper crown into the garden. 'Today,' she told the animals, 'we shall play at being Kings and Queens.'

She put the crown on her head. Then she put the curtain round her shoulders. 'Now I'm a queen,' she said. Little Monkey held the end of the curtain-robe, and Billie and the animals walked in solemn slow procession round the garden.

'When I'm Queen,' said Monkey, 'I shall walk to the top of the hill.'

'You can't be Queen,' said Woodley.

'Yes, I can!' said Monkey.

When it was Mr Milford-Haven's turn, he sat on the garden bench, and said, 'This is my throne.' Everyone came up to him, and bowed low.

'Now it's my turn!' said Woodley, and he put on the robe and crown, and ran round the garden so quickly that the procession couldn't keep up with him. In the end, everyone just sat down on the grass, and waited for him to come round the hill again.

'He must be the fastest King that ever lived!' said Mr Milford-Haven.

And then it was Monkey's turn. Billie tied the crimson robe round his shoulders, and put the crown on his head. It was rather big for him, and it nearly fell down over his nose. 'All bow to Queen Monkey!' he said.

'You can't be *Queen*, said Billie. 'Queens are girls. Boys are Kings.'

'I want to be Queen,' said Monkey. He gathered up his robe, and ran up a tree, and sat on a branch, looking down on everyone. 'I won't come down unless I can be Queen!' he said.

Monkey sat in the tree all day. When teatime came he said he wasn't hungry, and when bedtime came he said he wasn't sleepy. Billie went upstairs and sat the animals on the window sill, and snuggled down beneath the blankets. But she couldn't go to sleep, and after a while she got out of bed, and went to the window.

Monkey was still sitting on his branch. The moonlight shone on his crown, and he looked very small and lonely. Billie put on her dressing gown and her slippers and crept downstairs and out into the garden.

'Please come down!' she said, standing beneath Monkey's tree.

'I want to be Queen,' said Monkey.

'But you can't,' said Billie, 'because you're a boy. Boys are Kings.'

'It's not fair,' said Monkey.

'Yes it is,' said Billie. 'Some of us are girls, and some of us are boys. And you're a boy!'

'Which is best?' asked Monkey.

'They're each as good as one another,' said Billie. 'Kings and Queens – boys and girls.'

'All right!' said Monkey. 'I'll be King.'

He jumped from the tree, and Billie caught him in her arms. The crown slipped from his head, and went rolling over the moonlit grass. Billie picked it up for him, and set it straight on his head. Then together they went in solemn slow procession down the path, and as they went they looked up from time to time, to wave to all the animals on the window sill.

'Hail, King Monkey!' called the animals, as Billie and Monkey came into the bedroom. 'All hail the great King Monkey!'

When Monkey had walked three times round the bedroom he climbed into bed, and lay with his head on Billie's pillow. 'Goodnight, King Monkey!' said Billie, as she tucked him in.

'Goodnight, Queen Billie,' said Monkey – and he went to sleep, still wearing his crown.

The Sparrow

One day, in the garden, Mr Milford-Haven, Mrs Pinkerton-Trunks and Monkey decided that they would go for a long walk over the other side of the hill. Billie and Woodley waved goodbye to them, and when they had disappeared from sight, Woodley said, 'Come on, let's dance!'

But Billie had seen a little brown bird, hopping from branch to branch in a tree. 'What a nice little bird,' said Billie. 'I would like to have a little bird. He could sit in the wagon and play with us.'

'That is a sparrow,' said Woodley, 'and you can't make a sparrow sit in a *wagon*. You can't *play* with a sparrow. Let's dance!' And he went off over the grass, singing, 'Rum – tum – tiddle – I – rum – tum – tum.'

But Billie wanted to watch the little sparrow, and she lay on the grass, and looked up at the tree.

Woodley ran back, and looked at the bird; it was sitting on a branch, saying, 'Chirp, chirp, chirp.'

'Well, *I* could do *that*!' said Woodley.

'All right,' said Billie, sitting up, and looking at him. 'Do it!'

Woodley closed his eyes, and pursed his lips – but he couldn't go 'Chirp'. He said 'Wummp!' and 'Whup!' – but not 'Chirp!'

Billie lay down again, and looked at the sparrow. It flew from the tree and then it flew back again.

'Well, *I* could do *that*!' said Woodley. He marched up the hill, and when he reached the top, he ran a little way, leapt in the air – and fell down again. THUMP!

'Oh, Woodley!' said Billie.

'Perhaps it's easier to fly if you start from a tree,' said Woodley. So Billie helped him climb on to a low branch, and he sat there with his eyes closed for a moment. And then he jumped – and landed at her feet. THUD!

'Oh, Woodley!' said Billie.

Woodley lay in the grass, looking up at her. 'Dogs can't fly,' he said.

'I know,' said Billie.

She sat by his side, and watched as the sparrow picked a twig from the ground, and flew up with it into the tree. 'The sparrow's making a nest,' said Billie.

'I could make a nest!' said Woodley.

'In a *tree?*' asked Billie.

'Well, perhaps not in a tree,' said Woodley, 'but I could make a nest.' He jumped up, and began to collect bits of straw and twigs, which he put into the little wheelbarrow. When his nest was finished, he jumped in and sat down, looking very pleased with himself.

Then he raised his eyebrows. 'It's not very comfortable,' he said, ' . . . in fact, it's downright prickly!' Woodley jumped out of the wheelbarrow, and lay down at Billie's feet. He sighed, and put his nose on his paws.

'Look!' said Billie. 'The sparrow's pulled up a worm!'

'Right!' said Woodley, and he got up, and trotted across the garden, and began to dig. As he dug he threw up earth, and tufts of grass, and at last he reached the bone which he had buried the week before. He picked it up, and took it to Billie, and dropped it in her lap.

'There you are!' he said. 'It's yours . . . if that's

what you want – a pet who goes "Chirp," and who flies and makes nests, and digs things up . . . . '

'I don't,' said Billie. 'You're my pet.' She put her present on the grass, and gave Woodley a big hug.

The sparrow flew away over the garden. Billie and Woodley watched it go.

'That's the way with birds,' said Woodley. 'They like to come and go as they please.'

'I shouldn't like you to fly away,' said Billie.

'Neither should I,' said Woodley. 'Come on – let's dance!'

They were still dancing when Mr Milford-Haven, Mrs Pinkerton-Trunks and Monkey returned from their walk.

The Dancing Man

One day, when Billie and Woodley were sitting on the top of the hill, they saw Mrs Pinkerton-Trunks and Mr Milford-Haven standing by the hedge at the bottom of the garden. They were acting in a very strange way indeed. First Mrs Pinkerton-Trunks gave a little jump. Then Mr Milford-Haven gave a little jump. And then they both jumped up together. 'What *are* they doing?' asked Billie.

'They're trying to jump over the hedge,' said Woodley.

'Oh, Woodley,' said Billie. 'Don't be silly!'

But Woodley was right. When he and Billie went down to the bottom of the garden, both

94

Mrs Pinkerton-Trunks and Mr Milford-Haven were crouching as low to the ground as they could, and then jumping into the air.

'We're trying to jump over the hedge, dear,' said Mrs Pinkerton-Trunks. 'Monkey's on the other side, and we want to see who he's talking to.'

Billie went to the hedge and stood on tip-toes. But even standing on the very tips of her toes didn't make her tall enough to see who was on the other side of the hedge with Monkey.

'I'll wave to him, dear!' said Mrs Pinkerton-Trunks. 'I'll attract his attention!' She stretched up her long trunk, and called, 'Yoo-hoo! It's me! Who are you talking to, dear?'

But Monkey just went on talking and giggling on the other side of the hedge.

'Well, whoever it is with Monkey,' said Woodley, 'he hasn't got much to say for himself. He hasn't said a word!'

'I say!' said Mr Milford-Haven. 'The chap might not have much to say, but he's dancing rather well!'

Billie crouched by Mr Milford-Haven's side, and peeped through a gap in the hedge. And sure enough, there was an arm in an old jacket sleeve, waving to and fro; and there was the edge of the jacket, flapping in the breeze.

'I'm going to find out who this dancing fellow

is!' said Mr Milford-Haven. 'I'm going to *leap* over the hedge!'

Before anyone could stop him, he ran a little way, and leapt up into the air.

He came down on top of the hedge, with his head hanging over the field, and his back legs dangling in the garden. Then slowly, he slipped down, until he lay at Billie's feet.

'Who was Monkey talking to? asked Billie.

'Afraid I didn't see,' said Mr Milford-Haven. 'Fraid I closed my eyes.'

'Mr Milford-Haven,' said Billie, 'why don't we just climb through the gap in the hedge?'

'Good idea!' said Mr Milford-Haven. 'Don't know why we didn't think of that before!'

So Billie and the animals climbed through the gap in the hedge and into the field. Once they were in the field they began to run – but they had not run very far when they saw Monkey coming towards them. He was walking slowly, and dragging his feet.

'He wouldn't talk to me!' he said to Billie. 'I talked to *him*, but he wouldn't talk to *me*!'

Billie looked to where Monkey pointed a finger – and then she began to laugh. 'Oh, Monkey,' she said, 'of course he didn't talk. He's just an old scarecrow!'